T0128449

Ava gets her Wings

GEORGE-ANN
DUNOVANT

ILLUSTRATED BY:
KATHLEEN MILLER

Ava Gets Her Wings

iUniverse books may be ordered through booksellers or by contacting:

iUniverse
1663 Liberty Drive
Bloomington, IN 47403
www.iuniverse.com
844-349-9409

ISBN: 978-1-6632-2326-5 (sc)
ISBN: 978-1-6632-2327-2 (e)

Library of Congress Control Number: 2021909912

Print information available on the last page.

iUniverse rev. date: 08/24/2021

To my sweet Leo, Baby Dun, Kataleya, Skyler, Luke, Stella, TJ and Jaxon – Always remember that adventure is out there!

Ava sat on her bed. With a thud, she plopped herself onto the pile of things she wanted to bring with her. After all, this trip would be an extra special one. Visiting with Grandma was always a joy, but this time Ava would be going to Grandma's house. That meant she would have to take an airplane. Her very first plane ride!

As she thought about California, and all the fun things she and her Grandma would do, Ava began to make a list. "I'll need my new polka dot swimsuit, Mr. Gumdrop, this fabulous dress and my yellow sunshine purse. Perfect!"

"Hey Mom! Can you come check my suitcase please?"
"Sure Ava! Looks like you have a great start, but you'll need a couple more things. We will be spending five days with Grandma so you'll need an outfit for every day.

Choose your favorite pajamas, and don't forget the neck pillow you got last week. It'll be a long plane ride and you'll want to sleep comfortably. In the morning, before we leave, you can grab your toothbrush."

Ava hurried to her closet to pick out her favorite clothes.

She folded each outfit and packed it away.

She sat on her suitcase and with a tug, zipped it shut!

"Ava, we have a big day tomorrow.
It's time for you to go to bed."
"But Mom, I'm too excited to sleep!"
"Ava, please go brush your teeth and get snuggled up."
"Ok, Mom. Goodnight!"
"Goodnight Lovebug."

As the sun peeked through her window, Ava woke with a spring. BOING!
Her bag was packed and she was ready to go.
"Mom, Mom, Mom! Today's the day! Today I get my wings!"

"That's right Ava. Today is a big day for you, and I'm glad to see you this excited about it!" Ava's mom said with a smile.

She scarfed down her breakfast and ran to the door where her bag was sitting, ready for the car."

As they drove to the airport, Ava shook with excitement.
She looked up, imagining herself up in the sky, and smiled at
the thought of her first airplane ride. She reached over and
looked in her bag to double check that her coloring book,
snacks, and Mr. Gumdrop were still there.

When they got to the airport, the first thing they did was check in their bags. There was a bit of a line, so they had to wait a while. As they finally made it to the front of the line, Ava exclaimed, smiling at the airline clerk:
"Here! You can have my purple hippo bag!"
Her mom smirked and put her bag with Ava's.

Next, Ava and her mom had to go through security.

"Ava, finish the water in your bottle. Water is not allowed through security."

"But why mom?" asked Ava.

"Well, it's for safety Ava," replied Ava's mom.

"They don't want people to bring in dangerous liquids that could *look* like water."

"Oh, I get it!" And then Ava finished off the water in her bottle before they passed through.

Ava watched as her bag passed through the security machine. She saw her hat, her sunglasses, and her favorite teddy bear as they went by. Next, she walked through a metal detector machine so the security workers could make sure it was safe to board the plane.

"Can you raise your hands please?" asked the officer.

Ava raised her hands, and the woman passed a special bar in front of her body, scanning her from head to toe.

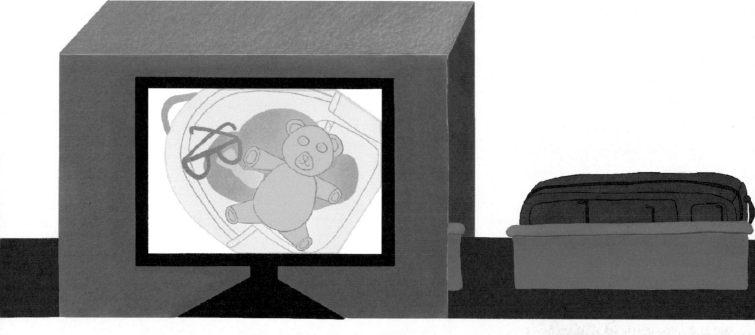

"We're heading to gate 28 Ava. If you look up you can see the numbers by the gates. Our flight is boarding already, so we have to hurry!" Ava's mom explained.
Ava and her mom raced to their gate.
Phew! Just in time!
There were only a few people left in the boarding line so Ava ran to get a spot before the doors closed.
"Can I have my ticket mommy?" asked Ava.
"Yes Ava, remember it's called a boarding pass. Here you go!"
"Have a safe flight!" said the man at the door.
"Thank you!" said Ava excitedly.

With a skip in her step, Ava held her mom's hand and walked onto the airplane. She was very happy to see that her seat was by a window.

"Mom, look! I'll be able to see when we go up!" Ava squealed. The plane rumbled to life, and the flight attendants began to make safety announcements. Ava clicked on her seatbelt and settled in for the long flight.

"It is important that you keep your seatbelt on during the flight because we may have some turbulence," said the flight attendant.

"What's turbulence?" asked Ava.

"It is when a plane flies through some bumpy air. The plane might shake, but don't worry, we'll be perfectly safe in here." said Ava's mom.

"Can I ever get up?" asked Ava.

"Of course, Honey." When the captain turns off the seatbelt sign, it means it is safe to get up."

When the plane began to move, Ava grabbed her mom's hand and squeezed.

"I'm scared," whimpered Ava.
"I know, but I'm right here with you, and remember, I love you!"

Ava smiled, and watched as the plane began to lift from the ground.

"I'm flying! I'm flying!" shouted Ava. "Yes Ava, you officially earned your wings today! Congratulations little bird."

Printed in the United States
by Baker & Taylor Publisher Services